Jonathan Bean

Big Snow

Farrar Straus Giroux

New York

"Mom," said David, "when will it snow?"

"I think soon," said Mom. "Why don't you help make cookies while you wait."

So David helped Mom make cookies. He took the sugar and raisins and flour from the cupboard. He measured out two cups of sugar. He measured one cup of raisins.

But then the flour, white and fine, made David think
of snow.

So he decided to check the weather.

Small flakes fell softly, white and fine.

"Mom," said David, "do you think it will snow taller than the grass?"

"I think so," said Mom. "Why don't you help clean the bathrooms while you wait to find out."

So David helped Mom clean. He put on the big yellow gloves. He sprayed the cleaner. He scrubbed with the heavy brush.

But then the suds, white and fluffy, made him think of snow.

So David decided to check the weather.

The flakes were lying, white and fluffy.

"Mom," said David, "do you think the snow will cover everything?"

"I think it could," said Mom. "Why don't you help me change sheets while you wait to find out. We have guests coming."

So David took sheets from the closet. He helped Mom take off the old sheets and put on the new.

But then the new sheets, white and cool, made him think of snow.

So David decided to check the weather.

The snow was covering everything, white and cool.

"Mom," said David, "is it going to be big snow?"
"It just might," said Mom. "Why don't you finish eating
lunch, and then take your nap while you wait to find out."

So David took his blanket and pillow from his bed. He curled up in the big armchair. He closed his eyes and began to dream. And he dreamt . . .

. . . that it was very big snow. That the snow fell heavily. That wild wind pushed flakes through window cracks. That it howled and shook the walls. That it roared and blew open all the doors and piled drifts around the house.

"Mom!" called David. "Is THIS big snow?"
"YES!" yelled Mom. "Help me clean up this huge mess!"

So David helped Mom clean up the snow. He tried to push the doors shut, but the drifts were too deep.

He tried to shovel away the drifts, but the snow just fell heavier. Suddenly, loud thumping shook the house!

David woke up. There was stomping at the door. It was Dad, home from work early. "Dad!" said David. "Is it very big snow?"

"Why don't you come find out for yourself?"

So David and Mom put on their winter coats. They wrapped long scarves around their necks. They pulled on warm hats and gloves.

Then David, Dad, and Mom went out to check on the big snow.

For my sister Susanna

Farrar Straus Giroux Books for Young Readers
175 Fifth Avenue, New York 10010

Copyright © 2013 by Jonathan Bean
Color separations by Bright Arts (H.K.) Ltd.
Printed in China by Macmillan Production (Asia) Ltd.,
Kowloon Bay, Hong Kong (supplier code 10)
Text designed by Jay Colvin
First edition, 2013
1 3 5 7 9 10 8 6 4 2

mackids.com

Library of Congress Cataloging-in-Publication Data
Bean, Jonathan, 1979–
   Big snow / Jonathan Bean. — First ed.
      pages   cm.
   Summary: "An excited and frustrated boy watches hopefully as wintry
weather develops slowly into a 'big snow.'"—Provided by publisher.
   ISBN 978-0-374-30696-0 (hardback)
   [1. Snow—Fiction.   2. Helpfulness—Fiction.   3. Mothers and sons—Fiction.]
I. Title.

PZ7.B3664Big 2013
[E]—dc23
                                                           2013000499

Farrar Straus Giroux Books for Young Readers may be purchased for business or
promotional use. For information on bulk purchases please contact Macmillan
Corporate and Premium Sales Department at (800) 221-7945 x5442
or by email at specialmarkets@macmillan.com.